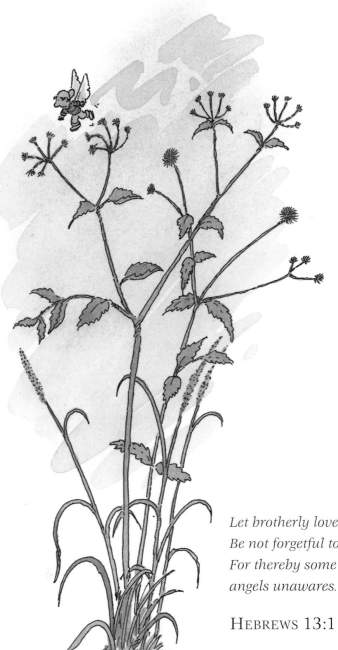

Let brotherly love continue.
Be not forgetful to entertain strangers:
For thereby some have entertained
angels unawares.

HEBREWS 13:1

for Madeline

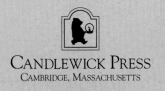

First U.S. edition 2002

Library of Congress Cataloging-in-Publication Data

Graham, Bob.
Jethro Byrd, fairy child / Bob Graham. —1st. U.S. ed.
p. cm.
Summary: Annabelle finds a family of fairies in
the cement and weeds, and they sing and
dance for her when she gives them tea.
ISBN 0-7636-1772-5
[1. Fairies—Fiction.] I. Title.
PZ7.G7516665 Je 2002
[E]—dc21   2001043534

10 9 8 7 6 5 4 3 2 1

Printed in Italy

This book was typeset in Stempel Schneidler.
The illustrations were done in watercolor and ink.

Candlewick Press
2067 Massachusetts Avenue
Cambridge, Massachusetts 02140

visit us at www.candlewick.com

CANDLEWICK PRESS
CAMBRIDGE, MASSACHUSETTS

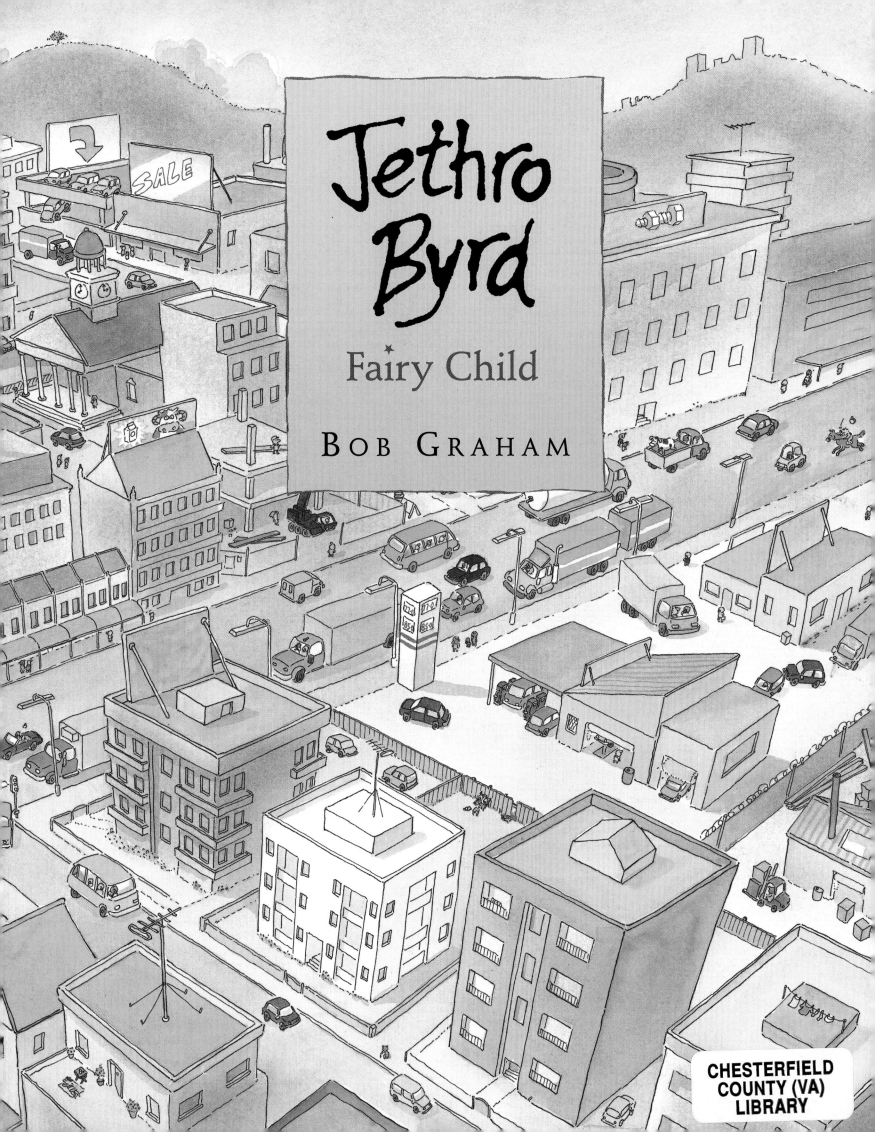

Jethro Byrd

Fairy Child

Bob Graham

Annabelle's dad had little time for fairies.
"Sadly, Annie," he said, "you won't
find fairies in cement and weeds —
as far as I know."

Annabelle had lots of time, and
every day she looked.

Even under her brother, Sam.

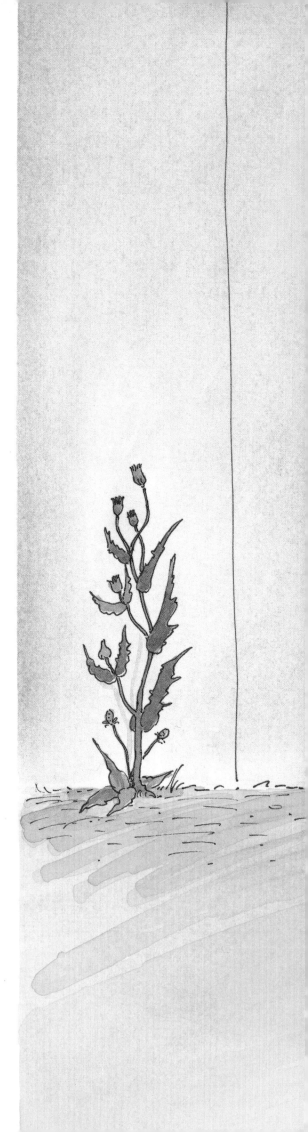

On Saturday,
    something bounced off the
gas station driveway and hit the fence,
    just where the weeds poked through. Annabelle parked her taxi.
And, with the fares uncollected, she went through to see.

There she met a boy —

as big as her finger.

His wings shivered in the breeze.

"Who are *you*?" she asked.

He hitched up his jeans,
flew onto a leaf, and wiped his nose
on the back of his sleeve.
"Jethro," he said. "Jethro Byrd . . . I'm a *Fairy Child.*"

What Annabelle saw next made her hold her breath.
An ice cream truck had dropped from the sky
and lay among the bottles and cans.
A family of fairies heaved
and pushed.

"Help us here, will you please?"
came a voice from the weeds.
Annabelle gently put out
her hand to set the truck
back on its wheels.

"Thanks," said the voice.
"And to whom do we owe
        this pleasure?"
Jethro's dad, Offin Byrd,
bowed deeply from the waist.
"He means, what's your name?"
        said Jethro.
"Annabelle," she said.

She let out her breath,
    making Jethro's mom's hair
    ripple like grass in a windy field.
    "What a lovely name,"
    said Lily Byrd. She kissed
    Annabelle on the cheek.

"That was one of Offin's
    not-so-good landings,"
    said Grandma Byrd.
    "Nearly hit the top of the
    gas station," added Lily.

Offin looked cross.
    "Well, we all agreed to come
    down for tea," said Offin.

"And to feed baby Cecily,"
    said Lily. Cecily was as
    big as a fingernail.

"My mom will make you tea," Annabelle said.

Lily's bells and bangles tinkled around her ankles.

"We would *love* to come to tea," she said.

"Let's go," said Jethro.

He did a Backward Air Skid over the fence.

"Mommy and Daddy, this is Jethro Byrd. He's a Fairy Child,
and his family have come to tea," said Annabelle.
"We must make them welcome, *and* make them tea," said Mom.

But she was looking the wrong way.

"Can you see Jethro, Daddy?"
Annabelle asked.
"I . . . I think I can, Annie.
I think he's . . .
ON THE FENCE?"

"Why doesn't my dad see you?"
Annabelle asked Lily.
"He's too grown up,
      Annabelle,"
   she replied.
"He doesn't have time for fairies."

"Do *you* have time for fairies, Mommy?"
      Annabelle asked.

"I've got time to make your friends
      tea," replied Mom. "Or maybe
         they have a magic wand?"

"Can you make magic?"
Annabelle asked.
The Byrds shook their heads.
"We just make hamburgers,"
said Offin Byrd.

Annabelle's mom
brought fairy cakes
and camomile tea
in fairy cups.

Annabelle served cake to
all her guests.
"Your mom's cakes are
charming," said Lily.
"Enchanting," said Grandma.
"Magic," said Offin.

They had second helpings and
refilled their cups with tea.

Only Annabelle's dad left his tea
untouched. His fingers moved
over his keyboard.

Clickety click,
clickety click,
clickety click.

Offin Byrd's foot began to tap.
He wiped his fingers and
reached for his bag.

Inside was a tiny fiddle,
dark red-brown like a chestnut.
As his bow hit the strings,
his fingers started flying.

That afternoon, for Annabelle,
    time stood still.

Offin played reels and he played jigs.
    Lily danced, with her charms and bracelets
        tinkling like wind chimes.

Jethro played a silver whistle,
    his sneakers sliding
                in cake crumbs.

Baby Cecily slept soundly
while Grandma sang a
slow, sad song,
clear as a church bell.

"No one sings sweeter
than a fairy," said Offin.
"Unless it's the lark
in the morning,"
Grandma replied.

"We must go,"
Offin said at last.
Annabelle's hands
flew to her face.
"But you can't," she said.

"Oh, you can't possibly," she added. "Go, I mean. Where to?"
"To make ice cream at the Fairy Travelers' Picnic," said Jethro.

"We go every year, and all my aunts go. . . . They all smell of roses and
hug me, and they have damp handkerchiefs, and the flies bite me,
and it's hot and itchy . . . and I have to run in the races,
and I always come in last.

And the prize for coming in last is . . .

a silly PLASTIC CUP.

And I don't want to go."

"Maybe Jethro could stay with *me*?" Annabelle said.

"We need you, Jethro," said Lily, "to help make the ice cream."

"And his aunts. They'll want to see Jethro again. It's been a whole year," said Grandma.

"Last year you won a beautiful cup," said Offin.

Jethro sulked a bit. Then he said,
"Maybe Annabelle could come with *us*?"
"I would love to come," said Annabelle.
"*Pleeease* take me with you."

Annabelle waited. The Byrd family whispered together.

Finally, Jethro took something off his wrist.

It sparkled silver in the late sun.

"It's for you, Annabelle," Offin said. "A fairy watch telling fairy time."

"And time goes by slowly for fairies," said Grandma.

"We thank you, Annabelle," said Lily, "for being kind and caring . . ."

"To strangers like us," added Grandma.

"And for the fairy cakes," said Jethro.

"We're sorry we can't take you with us," Lily went on.

"But fairies are this size, and humans are . . .
well, you're just too big."

"Will you come again?" Annabelle asked.
The fairy watch fit exactly around her finger.
"I'm sure we will," Jethro replied.
"Just don't forget to wind the watch."
"And keep looking," said Lily.
Annabelle carefully put the
truck on the driveway.

The engine coughed
and spluttered.
Wild flowers burst from the tailpipe.
And for those who had time to look,
the small truck gathered speed.
It bumped over the cracks in the concrete
and slowly left the ground like
a swan in flight.
The truck cleared the gas station roof and
headed west into the gathering dusk.

"Look at my ring, Daddy.
It's a fairy watch telling fairy time,"
said Annabelle.
"That's lovely, Annie," replied her dad.
He saw nothing, but Baby Sam did.
His fingers left cake and icing
on the glass.

"The Byrds said they were the nicest
fairy cakes they have ever eaten, Mommy," said Annabelle.
"Oh, *thank you*, Annabelle," replied her mom.

"I did find fairies in our cement and weeds, Mommy,"
said Annabelle.

And that night, the watch strapped tightly around her finger,
Annabelle saw more fairies.
From rich houses, poor houses,
playgrounds and parking lots, from under woodpiles
and high up in blackbirds' nests, from churches and
shop windows, and department stores after dark,
from mountains and valleys, back streets
and highways, from under hedges and bridges,
they rode in the moonlight to
the Fairy Travelers' Picnic.

And long after she fell asleep, their busy chattering
and the buzzing of their wings and their
faraway music filled her dreams.